FIELD MOUSE GOES TO WAR
TUSAN HOMICHI TUWVÖTA

by Edward A. Kennard   Hopi Text by Albert Yava

Illustrated by Fred Kabotie

Edited by Willard W. Beatty, Chief, Branch of Education (1936—1951)

Originally a Publication of the Branch of Education, Bureau of Indian Affairs, 1944

© 1999 Filter Press Palmer Lake, Colorado
Manufactured in the United States of America

ISBN: 0-86541-046-1

THE ARTIST

The Hopi Indian parents never used to keep records of their children's ages and birthdays. The artist was born during that period in the village of Shungopavy on Second Mesa. His family was among those who were opposed to the influence of the Government. When he was about six years of age this faction moved to Oraibi to join their allies. In less than a year they were forced out of the village and moved north to a location which later become Hotevilla. The following year the soldiers sent the people back to Shungopavy and took away the menfolks as prisoners.

Fred Kabotie's schooling began in spite of the wishes of his family. In the fall of 1915 he felt that school was of no value, nevertheless he attended under protest. Whether it was through the sympathetic understanding of the urgent need for education or as mere punishment to eliminate an annoyance on the part of the teacher, he was sent away to the Santa Fe Boarding School. The Indian policy, then, was to wean the Indian youth from his primitive life and to prevent his return to the blanket.

One day the fifth-grade class at Santa Fe was given an assignment to color the map of the United States. By chance, Mrs. Elizabeth DeHuff, wife of the superintendent, saw and liked the way Fred Kabotie used the colors in his map. Thenceforth, he was encouraged in his native art subjects and continued to paint, in spite of much adverse criticism. Mr. and Mrs. DeHuff were especially interested in Fred Kabotie, and he was greatly helped by their sympathetic understanding and advice and attended the city public high school. Lack of funds prevented him from continuing his education. He turned to his art work in order to support himself. From the first his work attracted attention, and he has illustrated a number of books and won many prizes for his paintings. Upon completion of his high school work, he was placed in museum work under Dr. Edgar L. Hewitt in Santa Fe where he continued his art work. Later he was commissioned by the Museum of the American Indian, New York City, to record authentic native Indian dances. Fred Harvey Company commissioned him to decorate the Indian Tower on the south rim of the Grand Canyon. Under the auspices of the Indian Arts and Crafts Board, he supervised and reproduced several murals from the prehistoric kivas of the abandoned Awatovi ruin for exhibit at the Museum of Modern Art, New York City. Other exhibitions have included: Art Museum of Santa Fe, Grand Central Art Galleries, Nelson and Rocknell Art Galleries, and the Denver Art Museum.

FIELD MOUSE GOES TO WAR

Most stories happened long ago
and far away.

But this story is different.
This story happened
right at Mishongnovi
and it was not
so very long ago.
At that time
the Mishongnovi people
were very rich.

TUSAN HOMICHI TUWVÖTA

Pai tuuwuchi wuuhakniqe pai hisat
hiniwtiqat yu'a'atangwu,
pu' yaaphaqamningwu.

Niq i' tuuwuchi alöngö.
I' tuuwuchi pai haipove yaniwti,
Musangnuve'e.
Pai qapas hisat yaw hiniwti.
Ephaqam Musangnup sinom
kyahak yeese.

1

2

Their storerooms were filled
with corn and beans
and squash and melons.
They had peaches and apples
and apricots.
They had many sheep and many goats
and many horses
and many cattle.
They even had burros.
Of course,
they had always had
corn and beans and squash
from the very Beginning.

Yuumokviyamui ang tuu'oyi
keevelmiq pichiwyungwu.
Pu' morivosi kuisivut ang
opom'iwta.
Paatnga pu' qawaiyo pu' meloni
wukovangawyungwa.
Yaw sipala'yungwa
mansaana'yungwa.
pu' söhöpsipala'yungwa.
Qanelmui, qaqapistui, qawaimui,
pu' waakasmui pokmui'yungwa.
Hikis yaw moropkomui'yungwa.
Owi paipi hisat qa'ö'yungwa,
morivosi'yungwa
paatnga'yungwa.

They had had peaches, apples,
and apricots
for so long
that they believed
they had always had them.
The old men could even
tell a story
to prove it.

But their proudest possessions
were their chickens.
Chickens were new.

Piw i' sipalaniqa pu' mansaana
pu' söhöpsipala
pai angqaq himu'yungwa.
Niq oovi pai hisatngahaqaq
himu'yungqe wuuwantota.
Hikis wuuwuyom hakimui amumi
tuutuwuchyangwu hakimui
tupchiwnayaniqe oovi'o.

Nikyang oovi imui suupwatui
hiitui imui kowaakomui
amumi unangwai'yungwa.
Puma kowaakom puuvuhum
amumi'i.

Old people remembered
   when they first came.
But they were very proud of them
   even if they were new.
Year after year
   there were more and more
chickens------
   for a while.

Then things changed.

Ima wuuwuyom navoti'yungwa
   hisat haqam mooti haqaq
   ökinayaqata.
Nikyang pai as pu' poktatakyang
   amumi pas unangwai'yungwa.
Yaasangoi ang aw wuuhaq
   naatkototangwu yaw keesiwa.

Pantaq yaw alöngtoti.

They began to lose their chickens.

They had a hard time.

At least,
  that is what
  they said.

Of course
  they had plenty
  of everything else.

So, they ate and ate
  and became fatter and fatter.

Kush hiniwtiq haqami
  kowaakomyangwu.
Paas kyaananvotya
  panqaqwangwu.
Nikyang pi as qahitaq okiwya.
Oovi pi suchep noonova
  nungwu pas a'ne wi'vaya.

But to hear them talk
   anyone would think
   they were going to starve
   the very next day
   if they lost
   one more chicken.

Yu'a'atote' supan chongostini
   kush hiitawat suuk taawat ep
   suuk kowaakot ngastatote'
   pan haqam yu'a'atotangwu.

8

On top of Corn Rock
   lived a hawk.
This hawk was the great enemy
   of the Mishongnovi people.
He was the one
   who was killing their chickens.
Day after day
   he killed
more and more chickens.
Day after day
   the chickens that were left
   became fewer and fewer.
In a little while
   there would be no chickens at all.

Niq yaw Qa'ötukwi ep
   kiisa ki'ta.
Niq i' kiisa yaw Musangnuptui
   a'ne tuwqa'am.
Pam yaw kush kowaakomui
   qöyanta.
Taatalöngqat ang yaw
   kowaakomui qöyanta.
Taatalöngqat paapu hikiyom
   peetingwu.

Hisavoniq ke so'on haqam
   kowaakoni.

The people were worried.
The people were troubled.
All they talked about
    was that hawk
    who was killing their chickens.
The boys were always making plans
    to kill the hawk.
But nothing came of their plans
    and the chickens were killed
    just the same as before.
The women told one another
    how many chickens
    they had lost.
They told one another
    how scarce eggs were.

Sinom yaw qahaalaya.
Yaw sinom wuwnit aw öki.
Kiisatsa yaw sosoyom yu'a'tota,
    pam kowaakomui qöyantaq'ö.
Tootim yaw suchep nanawinya
    hin niinayaniqa'e.
Haktonsa yaw nanawinya suchep
    kowaakomui yaw qöyanta.
Momoyam naa'awintota
    hiisa kowaakovokmui
    ngastatote' pangqaqwangwu.
Pu' piw nöhu yaava'iwma.

10

They told
      their husbands and fathers
      and nephews and sons
      to kill the hawk.
The men agreed.
They knew it was up to them.
They had meetings.
They went to the kivas
      and they talked all night.
They talked all night
      for many nights.
They made plans, too.

But they did not kill the hawk.

Taataktui ayalalawa
      tuwqai niinayaniqata.
Taatakt hu'wawatota.
Navoti'yungwa kush pi hin
      qapumayani.
Pu' yaw chovaltingwu.
Kivanawit tookyep yu'a'atotangwu.
Pas qasuus tookyep yu'a'atota,
      pu' nanawinya.

Nikyang qaniinaya.

The Village Chief and the Crier
   had a meeting.
They knew
   that their people were troubled.
They smoked and talked
   and prayed.
Something had to be done.

They smoked and talked
   and prayed some more.
They knew what had to be done.
The hawk had to be killed.

Everyone knew that.

Pu' yaw Mongwi'am
   Cha'akmongwi amum
   tuwat naami pitu.
Pu' puma navoti'ta
   sinomat qahaalayaq'ö.
Yaw chochongot yu'a'atangwu.
Pu' piw yaw as naawaknangwu.

So'on as qahintani.
Panchaki yaw chochongot,
   yu'a'atangwu,
   pu' as naawaknangwu.

Pai as sen hintani hin as
   kiisat niinani.

12

The men and women
    and boys knew it.
Even the children knew it.
But no one knew how.

A little field mouse lived
    on the south side of the village.
He heard all about
    all the trouble
    the Mishongnovi people
    were having.
He felt very sorry for them.
He felt so sorry that he decided
    to kill the hawk for them.

Taatakt, momoyam, tootim,
    pu' hikis chachayom nutum
    pan wuuwantota.
Nikyang qahak hin
    niinayaniqat navoti'ta.

Niq yaw tavangqöviq
    haq tuwat ki'ta.
Pam yaw sosok nanvota
    sinom Musangnuve hiitaq
    qahaalayaq'ö.
Pas amungem qahaalaiti.
Pas yaw qahaalaitiqe
    amungem kiisat niinaniqe
    pasiwna.

One night
   he picked up his tobacco pouch
   and went to the house
   of the Village Chief.
He knocked on the door.
"Come in," they called.
He went in.
The Village Chief
   was surprised to see him.
"Sit down there.
Eat," he told the mouse.
The mouse sat down
   and ate a meal of
   corn mush and boiled beans.

Pu' oovi hisat mihiq
   pipmoki kwusut
   mongwit kiyat aw wuuvi.
Ep yaw pitu.
Pu' yaw paki'a'awnaya.
"Yungya'ai," yaw aw kitota.
Pu' yaw aw paki.

Paas taviya.
Niq Mongwi hin kush wuuwa.
Pu' qatu'a'awna.
"Qatu'ui. Nösa'ai," yaw aw kita.
Niq yaw kush Tusan Homichi.
Yaw nösa.
Morivoskwivit nit paatupsikit
   yaw nösa.

14

When he had eaten enough
he moved away
from the bowls of food
and sat against the wall.
Finally the Village Chief said,
"I guess you had some reason
for coming here."
"Yes," said the field mouse.
"But wait until we have
a smoke first."

The field mouse took out
his tobacco pouch.
He took out his pipe.

Öyit ayo'hoyo.
Pu' tuupelvo taachi.
Paasat Mongwi tuuvingta,
"Owi. Hinniq um pitu?"
"Owi," kita yaw Tusan Homichi.
"Haaki, ason itam chochongotni."

Pu' Tusan Homichi chongoi
horoknat ang tangata.

16

He filled the pipe
　and lighted it.
He smoked and offered it
　to the Village Chief.
The Chief smoked a while
　and passed it back.
When they had finished smoking,
　the Chief asked again,
　"Why have you come here?"
Then the mouse told him,
　"I feel very sorry
　for you and your people.
I pity you because
　this hawk is killing
　all your chickens."

Pu' uwikna.
Naalös ang chochonat
　Mongwit aw tavi.
Pu' Mongwi tuwat chochongo.
Sowat yaw aw tavi.
"Ta'ai,hinniq um wainuma?"
Mongwi piw aw kita.
Pu' Tusan Homichi kita,
　"Owi nu' ungem pas qahaalayi.
Usinmui amungem qahaalaitiqe
　nu' ung okwatuwa,
　ancha i' kiisa
　umukowaakomui qöyantaq'ö."

17

The Village Chief said,
    "Is that so?
What do you plan
    to do about it?"
"I have been thinking
    about it.
I shall try to do
    something for you.
I shall try to kill
    the hawk for you."

The Village Chief just looked
    at the little mouse.

Pu' Mongwi lavaiti.
"Ha'owi?" yaw kita.
"Niq hintani?
Hin um wuuwa?"
"Owi nu' wuuwanta.
Niq nu' umungem aw
    tuwantani niinaniqayu."

Panis yaw Mongwi aw yori.

In his heart he was thinking,
    "This little mouse
    cannot do anything.
He is too small.
Surely he cannot
    kill that hawk.
After all, the Crier and I
    don't know how.
The men don't know how.
The boys have failed."
But he did not say that
    to the mouse.
Instead, he said,
    "All right. Thank you."

Unangpe wuuwa,
    "So'onpi i' hisaihoya,
    nikyang hita niinani.
Sokpi hisaihoya.
So'onpi kiisat niinani.
Pu' piw tuwqa'ata.
Pi hikis Cha'akmongwi niq nu'
    hin niinaniqe qanavoti'ta.
Hikis tootim qaniinanaya."
Pai as yan wuuwat
    qa'aw pan lavaiti.
"Ancha'ai. Kwakai," paasat kita.

Then the mouse told him,

"Tomorrow you will

announce it.

The time will come

in four days.

Until that time

the women can be getting ready.

The third day will be totokya-

the day of preparation-

and the fourth day

will be the dance day.

Then I shall kill this enemy.

So, having these thoughts in mind,

we shall approach that day."

Paasat piw Tusan Homichi lavaiti.

"Qaavo taalawvaq

um tuu'a'awnani.

Naalötoq aw pituni.

Niq pangsoq haqami

ima momoyam na'sastotani.

Paitoq totokyani.

Naalötoq aw talöngiwtani ep

nu' tuwqat niinani.

Oovi itsa itam wuuwankyakyang

aw hoyoyotani."

The Village Chief was happy.
The little mouse spoke just right.
Maybe he could kill their enemy.
He told the mouse,
    "Tomorrow morning the Crier
    will announce it."
"All right. We'll go to sleep,"
    the mouse said.

He picked up his pipe
    and his tobacco bag
    and went home.

Niq yaw Mongwi haalaiti.
Tusan Homichi su'an lavaiti.
Pai sen mongvasni niinaniq'ö.
Yan lavaiti ,"Qavo'o
    i' Cha'akmongwi pan cha'lawni."
"Niq oovi itam pan
    unangvasikyang tokwisni,"
    kita piw homichhoya.

Nit pipmoki kwusut
    panq nima.

After the mouse had gone,
   the Chief picked up
   his tobacco bag and pipe
   and went to the Crier's house.
He knocked on the door.
"Come in," he was told.
When he went inside
   they offered him food,
   but he ate only a little.
He was too excited to eat much.
He filled his pipe.
He lit it and
   smoked four times.

Pu' tuwat paasat Mongwi
   pipmoki kwusut
   Cha'akmongwit kiyat aw'i.
Ep pitut pöövönga.
  "Yunga'ai," kitota.
Pu' aw paki.
Niq yaw tunus'a'awnaya.
Yaw nöösa pai hiisaq.
Yaw wuwniwui akw qahaalaiqe
   oovi hiisaq nöösa.
Pu' chongoi tangatat
   pu' uwikna.
Naalös angq chochonat

He passed the pipe
   to the Crier.
The Crier took it, saying,
   "My father."
The Crier smoked four times
   and passed it back.
The Kikmongwi said, "My father,
I think we have done our part
   with this smoke.
Now why have you come?"
The Village Chief answered,
   "I have come because of
   the trouble we are having.
You know what that trouble is.
Tonight I had a visitor.
This visitor offered his help.

pu' Cha'akmongwit aw tavi.
"Ina'ai," yaw aw kita.
Pu' tuwat Cha'akmongwi
   chochonat aw ahoi tavi.
"Iti'i," kita aw Kikmongwi.
"Pai itam pasiwna.
Pai hovakuiti.
Owi, hinniq um pitu?"
Paasat tuwat Mongwi lavaiti.
   "Owi, yep himu qa'antaqa
   hiniwma pai um navoti'ta
   himuniq'ö.
Nu' pu' haki pichina.
Pam itamungem naa'oini.
Panniq pitu.

23

He set a date.

He told me to have you announce

    that the great event

    will take place in four days.

The third day will be totokya

    and the fourth day

    will be the dance day.

On that day

    he will kill our enemy.

So with happy hearts

    let us prepare

    for that day."

Niq tokilta.

Nui ayata um cha'lawni

    naalötoq aw talöngwiwtani.

Paitoq pas an totokyani.

Qavongvaq tikiveni.

Niq ep tikive itatuwqai

    niinani.

Niq oovi itam haalaikyakyang

    aw hoyoyotani."

Yan haqam lavaiti.

The Crier asked,
  "Who is the one
  who will help us?"
"It is that dirty little field mouse
  who lives on the south side
  of the village."
At first
  the Crier wanted
  to laugh.
Then he was angry.
Next he wondered
  if the Chief
  had lost his mind.

"Haq'i," yaw kita Cha'akmongwi.
"Pai i' Tusan Homichi,
  tavangqöviq ki'taqa,"
  yan lavaiti.
Mooti as Cha'akmongwi naaninit
  pai qapanti.
Nit aw wuuwaqe ichivuti.
Pu' sen itamongwi qahoonaqti
  niqe oovi hiisaqhoyat
  wuwniyat hu'wa

Finally, he said,
  "All right. I will give
  the message to our children."
There was nothing else
  he could say.
There was nothing else
  he could do.
Then the Crier
  filled and lit his pipe
  and offered it
  to the Chief who said,
  "My child."
The Chief smoked four times
  and passed back the pipe
  to the Crier who said
  "My father."

Paasat nawista natuu'a'awnani.
Kush pi hita achve lavaitini.
Pu' kush piw put ep hintini.
Pu' yaw paasat Cha'akmongwi
  chongoi takchokyat
  naalös angq chochonat
  Mongwit aw tavi.
"Iti'i," kita yaw Mongwi.
Pu' Mongwi tuwat chochongot
  sowat aw tavi.
"Ina'ai," kita yaw Cha'akmongwi.

The Crier smoked four times.
When he had finished
   the Chief said,
   "Thinking only of this great event
   let us go to sleep."
The Village Chief went home.
He went to bed.
But the Crier
   stayed up all night.
Four times he went out
   and looked at the stars.
The fourth time
   was just before sunrise.
Then he made the announcement
   from the housetop.

Paasat yaw naalös chochonat
   tuwati.
Pu' lavaiti, "Ta'ai.
Yaapi itam aw talöngwiwtaniqatsa
   wuuwantikyakyang
   unangvastotani.
Itam oovi tokwisni."
Pangqaq Mongwi yaw nima.
Pu' puwto.
Niq tuwat Cha'akmongwi qapuwi.
Tookyep toktaita.
Naalös ipo yamat
   hotonqamui aw poota.
Naalöstiqat ep naat qatawat
   yamaq
   kiichongaq cha alawu.

The little mouse heard it
   and was happy.
The people heard it
   and laughed.
The first day the men went
   far to the north
   to bring back wood.
The women shelled corn.
All day they laughed
   at the little mouse.
They told one another
   he was too small
   to kill the hawk.

Supasat   homichhoyat
   kush   taataiqe   navota.
Niq   yaw   haalaiti.
Pu' tuwat   sinom   nanaptaqe   chuiti.
Qavongvaq   tootim   hoopoq
   komokwisa
   pu'   momoyam   humitiva.
Teevep   homichit   aw   chuchuya.
Naanami   lavaitaqe,
   "Kush   pi   hin   pam   hisaihoya
   nikyang   kiisat   niinani."

They said
  he could not succeed
  when they themselves
  had failed.
The second day
  the men hauled water
  from springs
  far below the village.
The women ground corn
  all day long.
The second day they were angry.
They were angry
  at the mouse
  and the Village Chief
  and the Crier.

So'on pi pasiwni antini.
Hikis pi naapyakyang qaniinaya.
Pu' piw qavongvaq taatakt
    kuyi'oilalawa paangaq'ö.
Pu' momoyam ngumantiva.
Teevep yaw ngumantota.
Ep yaw ichivu'iwyungwa.
Homichit aqw ichivutoti.
Pu' Mongwit piw aqw'a.
Piw Cha'akmongwit aqw'a.

They said that

    the dirty little mouse

    was crazy to even try

    to kill the hawk.

They said that

    the Village Chief

    was crazy to even listen

    to the mouse.

They said that

    the Crier was crazy

    to set the date.

They said that

    all their hard work

    would be for nothing.

The third day was totokya.

The men butchered sheep.

"So'on pi Tusan Homichi

    hisaihoya nikyang

    kiisat niinani."

"Pu' Mongwi ke yaw

    hoonaq'iwtaqe ke oovi

    put hisaqhoyat aw tuqaivasta."

"Pu' piw Cha'akmongwi an haqam

    hoonaq'iwtaqe pan haqam

    cha'alawu."

Pu' pan lavaitoti.

"Qahita oovi itam maksonlalawa,"

    kitota piwu.

Paiyis talöngwiwtaqat ep totokya.

Taatakt qanelqöqya.

31

They killed many sheep.
The women made piki
   and pik'ami, too.
They worked all day long.
It was a great day
   of preparation.
The third day they wondered.
They wondered
   if the mouse
   had some great power.
They wondered
   if the Chief knew
   the mouse had power.

Wuuhak qöqya.
Pu' tuwat momoyam pas an
   piktotat pu' pik'amya.
Qa'a'saqalya is pi pavan
   aw talöng'iwtaniq'ö.
Ep yaw wuuwantivaya.
Wuuwantotaqe ke sen
   Tusan Homichi a'ne himu'u.
Pu' wuwantota sen pi yaw
   Mongwi navoti'ta
   a'ne himuniq'ö.

33

They told one another
   it could not be helped.
It had been decided.
It had been announced.
They would have
   to do their part.

Naanami yaw kitota,
   "Paipi nuwupi'i."
Pan hapi pasiwti.
Pu' pan cha'lawiwqa.
Nawis tuwat naape apitotini.

On totokya
   the little mouse
   was getting ready, too.
He took a greasewood stick.
With his knife
   he sharpened it
   to a point.
He made the point very sharp.

Totokpe Tusan Homichi yaw
   yuuyuwsi tuwati.
Teepsoyat kwusut poyoi akw
   chukutotoina.
A'ne chukutai.

From inside his kiva
    he dug a hole
    under the ground
    that came out
    quite a distance
    from his kiva.
That night
    when everyone in the village
    went to sleep
    the little mouse
    stayed up all night long.
He smoked all night.

Pu' kivai aapi atkyava
    yaw hangwantiva.
Yaap haqam oomi höta.
Tookyep sinom tookyaq
    tuwat hangwantumlai'ta.
Pas an piw tuwat toktai'ta.
Tookyep chochongo.

Three times he went out
and looked at the stars.
The third time
when he came back
he took out his feathers
and his war paints
and other things.
He began to dress himself.
On top of his head
he tied the tip
of a feather
from an eagle's wing
with a downy feather
from an eagle's breast.
He tied them with cotton.

Paiyis kivai angq yama.
Pu' sotui amumi pootangwu.
Paiyistiqat ep na'chi horokna.
Pu' nakwai pu' tuumata
pu'hita yuwsi kivaqe
yan yuuyuwsi.
Mooti hurunkwata.

With white clay
    he painted his cheeks
    and the right side
    of his forehead.
He put the white
    on his arms and chest
    and on his thighs and legs.
He painted a black mark
    across his eyes.
He put on his kilt.
He tied shells
    from the ocean
    around his right wrist.
He got his bow
    and his war club.

Pu' yaw tuumat qömata.
Pu' putngatwat angq
    tuumat qalekmata.
Pu' tuumat akw mai
    pu' tawichqavi
    pu' hokyai pang lelewi.
Pu' yaw yalaqömata.
Pu' pitkunta pu' sochapmaponta
    pu' hoomachvonta.
Pu' hootngai ikwilta.
Pu' owavikya'ungwai
    enang kwusu.

He took off his moccasins.
Then he sat down
   and thought about his songs.
Dressed like a real warrior,
   he thought like a real warrior.
The next day was the great event.
The next day was the dance day.
All the Mishongnovi people
   got up early
   and washed their heads.
They dressed their children
   in their newest clothes.

Yaw qatochkyango.
Pas yuwsit pu' qatuptu.
Pu' wuuwantiva tawi ang'a.
Pas yaw yuwsiqe pas qaleetaqat
   an yaw yuwsiqe wuuwa.
Qavongvaq aw pas
   wukotalöngwiwta.
Ep tikiveni.
Musangnup sinom su'ich taayungwa.
Aa'asya pu' yuuyaha.
Timui yuwsinatota.

41

The men wore their

    brightest headbands,

    their silver belts,

    and their turquoise necklaces.

The women wore

    their bracelets and rings

    of silver and turquoise

    and their brightest shawls.

Visitors came

    from all the other villages.

They came on horseback,

    on burros,

    in wagons,

    and on foot.

They were all dressed up, too.

Taatakt warani yuuyaha

    tukwapnguntota pu' sipkwewai

    kwewtota.

Pu' momoyam tuwat tangavi

    pu'siipmasmi yuuyaha.

Pu' usi usitota.

Kiyavaqvit öki kiiyangaq'ö.

Qawaimui akw pu' momorotui akw

    pu' qaretamui akw

    pu' haqawatnaapya.

Puma piw yaw a'ne yuuyaha.

43

They came to see

    their friends and relations.

They came to talk

    and to joke.

They came to eat

    piki and pik'ami,

    somiviki and noqkwivi.

Boys came to smile

    at the girls.

But most of all

    they came

    to see the dance.

Everyone wondered

    what was going to happen.

Puma kwachmui pu' sinomui

    pootawiskyakyang timai öki.

Petu pai kivung'öki.

Petu nöswisa pik'ami nit piki

    pu' nöqkwivi niitiwta.

Pu' ima tootim tuwat

    mamantui oovi öki,

    sasaiyaniqe oovo'o.

Pas yaw noovi a'ne pu'

    wuhakniqani timai'öki.

Sosoyom wuuwantota hin pa

    hiniwti.

Some laughed.
They said
    the little mouse
    was too small
    to kill the hawk.
Others were angry.
They said
    it was foolish
    to set the date
    and have the dance
    and do all the work
    for nothing.
They said
    the visitors
    were laughing at them.

Petu chuchuya pi
    Tusan Homichi hisaihoya.
"So'on pi chaihoya nikyang
    kiisat niinani, kitota."
Pu' petu ichivu'iwyungwa.
"A'newaq qachitota tumala
    paisoq qahita oovi maksontota,"
    kitota petu'u.
Petu lavaitaqe kiyavaqvit paisoq
    itamumiq   chuchuya.

But a few did not laugh
   and they were not angry.
They said,
   "Wait and see.
Maybe that mouse
   has some great power."

By noon there was a big crowd.
They all gathered around
   the little mouse's kiva.
The people were surprised.

Niq tuwat hikiyom qachuchuya,
   pu' qa'ichivu'iwyungwa.
"Haaki," kitota.
"Pai sen mongvasni.
Sen homichhoya a'ne himu'u."

Tawanasap'iwmaq qa'aan'ewaq
   sinom Tusan Homichit
   kivayat aqw chovalti.
Sinom kyaataiyungwa.

Tied to the ladder
  was a real warrior's standard.
It was a bow standard.
It looked like
  it was going to be
  a war dance.
Just at noon
  the little mouse
  came out.

Yaw qaleetaqat na'chi'at
  saakpe leechiwta.
Yaw awtana'chi.
Yan yaw yorikya.
Sutawanasave Tusan Homichi
  yaw yama.

He danced right in front
   of his kiva.
He danced all by himself.
He was dressed
   just like
   a real warrior.
The people laughed at him.
As he danced
   he sang this song.
"The hawk kills chickens.
The hawk kills rabbits.
But the hawk won't kill
   Tusan Homichi.
Monster Hawk will surely die."

Pas an kivai aapi
   taak wunima.
Sunala yaw nöönönga.
Pas qaleetaqat an yuwsi'ta.
Niq sinom aw chui'ti.
Wunima yaw tawkyang
   kiisat yaw tawsoma.
"Kiisa kowaako maakya.
Kiisa taap maakya.
Pankyang so'on um nui niinani .
Umsa mokni."

The hawk was watching
    from the top of Corn Rock.
When he heard the song
    he became angry.
Just as he stretched his wings
    to fly down,
    the little mouse
    went back into his kiva.
The little mouse came out again.
This time he danced
    farther away from his kiva.
He sang his song again.
But all the time
    he sang and danced,
    he watched the hawk.

Qa'ötukwingaq kiisa
    aw tunatyawta.
Tawiyat navotqe
    pas yaw ichivuti.
Panis masavuyaltiq
    Tusan Homichi kivai aqw
    supki.
Piw yaw yama.
Piw wunima kivai aapi'o.
Taatawtikyang
    pas tunatyawkyango
    kiisat aw'i.

51

As he danced
  he went closer
  and closer
  to the opening
  of his kiva.
This time the hawk
  flew away from Corn Rock.
But the little mouse
  quickly ducked into his kiva
  and the hawk flew back.

Pai hihin yaavo pu' pitu,
  wunimaqa'e.
Pan wunimantikyang
  kivai aqw hoyoyotima.
Piw kiisa puuyalti
  qa'ötukwingaqö.
Piw yaw Tusan Homichi supki.
Kiisa ahoi aqw chokilti
  qa'ötukwimiq'a.

The third time
  the little mouse came out
  he walked still farther
  away from his kiva.
He began to dance there.
He sang his song.
But as he danced
  he came closer and closer
  to his kiva.

Paayistiqat ep piw yama.
Pasat piw hihin yaavotit
  wunimantiva.
Piw taatawtiva.
Piw ahoi kivai aw hoyoyotima.

This time the hawk
    swooped down,
    but just as he
    was about to catch him,
    the mouse ducked
    into his kiva.
The people gasped.
They were frightened.
They were sure the hawk
    was going to kill him.

Naat wunimaq kiisa wuuku.
Sumataq Tusan Homichi
    qatuiqawvani
    kiva höchiwai aqw'a.
Sinom chaachawnakyang
    tu'qawyungwa,
    Tusan Homichit engemi.

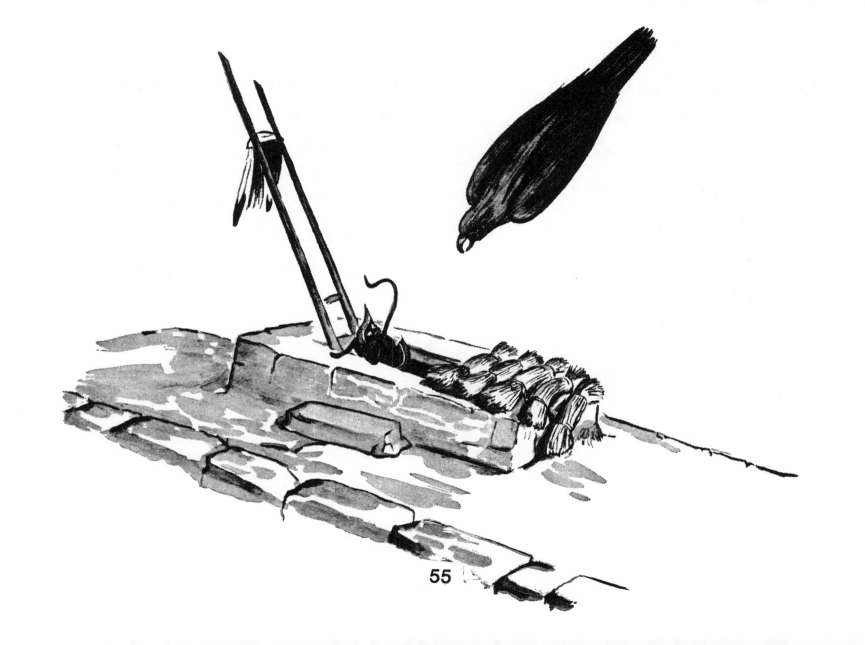

55

They told one another,
   "If that dirty little mouse
   does not stay close
   to his hole,
   the hawk will
   surely kill him
   next time."

Down in his kiva
   the little mouse was very busy.

"Suyan kiisa niinani pu'u,"
   kitota yaw naanami.
"Pai kivai ahaipove wunime'
   pai so'onqa tuiqawvani."

Pas oovi hihin tuiqawva
   kivami haqami.
Paisoq poosi.

He took his stick,
    his sharp-pointed
    greasewood stick,
    and crawled along
    the hole he had dug.

Paasat kivapeq pisoq teepkoi
    kwusut ep tokinen
    hötaqe pangsoq paki.

When he came to the opening
    he pushed up the stick
    so the sharp point stood up
    right next to the hole.
Then he crawled back
    to his kiva.
He came out again.
He walked far away
    from his kiva.
When he came to the other
    hole next to the pointed stick,
    he stopped.
He began to dance there.

Pu' kivai aapi yaap hötaqe
    pangq teepkoi chööqökna
    höchit aqlaq.
Paasat aqw paki.
Pu' yaw piw yama.
Pu' yaavo kwilalaiku kivai angq.
Pu' höchiwai pep
    teepko'at chööqökiwtaqat
    pep wunuptu.
Paapi wunimantiva piwu.

59

The people were surprised.

The mouse was so foolish.

He was too far away.

It was just what they expected.

But they watched him dance, anyway.

This is what
   the little mouse sang
   while he danced,

"Tusan Homichi,
   Tusan Homichi,
   He has whiskers
   sticking from his nose."

Then he gave his war cry.

Nikyang ancha timaya.

Sinom kush hin aw wuuwaya.
   pep wunimantiva?"

"Pu hinnoq pas yaavoq kwilat

Niq it yaw tawlawu.

"Tusan Homichi
   Tusan Homichi
   Yayaqangaq hömi chiproyungwa.

Yayaqangaq hömi chiproyungwa."

Sootapnaat pu' yaw kipoqtöqti.

It sounded just like a mouse squeak,
    but it was his war cry, anyhow.
As he danced
    he lifted the bow
    in his left hand,
    and he lifted his war club
    in his right hand
    each time he turned around.
Then he sang,
    "The hawk kills chickens.
The hawk kills rabbits.
But the hawk won't kill
    Tusan Homichi.
Monster Hawk will surely die."

Pai homich'ewaq töqti
    nikyang pai tuwat kipoqtöqti.
Wunimakyang hoomachvoi iita
    pu' yaw piw tunipi iita,
    angsakis namtö pantingwu.
Piw tawkuina.
"Kiisa kowaako maakya.
Kiisa taap maakya.
Pankyang so'on um nui niinani.
Umsa mokni."

The hawk became very angry.
But he was sure
   he would kill the mouse this time.
He was too far away
   from his kiva.
When the little mouse
   finished his song,
   he shook his war club
   up at the hawk
   and just stood there.

Yaw kush kiisa ichivuti.
Pu' pi pas suyan
   Tusan Homichit niinani.
Panis Tusan Homichi tawi
   sootapnaq'ö
   tunipi aw wiwila.
Pas suchikwingwunuptut
   piw aw wiwila.

The hawk swooped down
   from his high perch
   straight for the mouse.
Just as he reached him
   the little mouse
   jumped into the hole.
The hawk did not see
   the sharp-pointed stick.

Pantiq pu' yaw kiisa wuuku piwu.
Qamu yaw pu' qangu'ani,
   oovi aw haikyalaq'ö
   Tusan Homichi supki
   höchi aqw'a.
Kiisa kush yaw pangqaq
   teepko a'ne chukutaqa
   ichiwtaqat qatuwai'ta.

He landed right on it
   and cut open his throat.
He rolled over dead.
That is how the little mouse
   got rid of the monster
   for the people.

At first the people
   could not believe
   their own eyes.
Then they were happy.

Su'aq tunusmoki aqw chöqö.
Sukwaptuki.
Panis wa'ö'öiku.
Yan haqam yaw a'ne tuwqat
   niina sinmui amungem.

Mootiniq sinom pas qatuutupchiwa
   aw yorikyakyango.
Pu' pas haalaya.

65

The Village Chief
  came down to the mouse's kiva.
The Crier came with him.
They both wore kilts
  and had their hair hanging loose
  down their backs.
While the little mouse
  stood in front of his kiva,
  the Chief and the Crier
  gave him prayer sticks
  and prayer feathers
  and sacred corn meal.

Pu' yaw Mongwi'am nakwsu
  kivami'i.
Cha'akmongwi yaw amum.
Naama yaw sakwavitkunma.
Angapuyawma.
Tusan Homichi kivach'oviq
  wunuwtaqat aw'i.
Mongwi niq pu' Cha'akmongwi
  paho'ini yaw maqa,
  hoomat enanga

Then the Chief smoked over him
and the Crier sprinkled him
with medicine.
Then all the women of Mishongnovi
started for his kiva.
The old women, the young women,
and the girls
all started down
to the mouse's kiva.
They made a long line,
and each had something
on her back.

Pu' yaw Mongwi chongot
ang poyakinta.
Pu' Cha'akmongwi aw hoomakyang
pu' maakwa.
Pu' ima Musangnup momoyam
nankwusa.
Soso akw pu' momoyam
pu' mamant puma sosoyom
aw haani kivayat aw'i.
Pas yaw se'elhaq wupawisiwta.
Sosoyom noovat ikwiwwisa
pu' ini'wisa.

At his kiva
    the women gave him
    piki and pik'ami,
    somiviki and noqkwivi,
    and many other kinds of food.
They piled it all around his kiva.
That is how they paid him
    for his courage
    and his cleverness
    in killing the hawk.

Kivayat aw ökit'a
    momoyam pikita, pik'amta,
    pu' nöqkwivita,
    pu' wuuyakipwat nösiwqat
    aw pangalaya.
Yan haqam yaw Tusan Homichit
    aw naakwaiya,
    amungem tuwqat
    niinaq oovi'o.
Kush a'ne taak'unangwa.
Pai yan'i.

THE HOPI ALPHABET

The following information about the Hopi alphabet and its use should prove helpful to one familiar with the English language. After each letter, an example of the sound represented is given in a Hopi word, followed by an example of the same sound in an English word. In cases where English lacks a particular sound the nearest approximation to it is given.

VOWELS

a	mana	(girl)	father
e	pep	(there)	met
i	iti'i	(my child)	machine
o	chongo	(pipe)	open
u	puhu	(new)	put

The u of Hopi is a much closer u than in the English word, put. It is at the opposite extreme from the rounded u in a word like rule, and instead of the lips being rounded, they are retracted. The sound of the u in English put is intermediate in relation to the u in rule and the Hopi u.

ö	löqö	(pine tree)	purple

This sound is the same as the ö in the German word schön. It is similar to the sound in the English words purple or third, as they are pronounced in southern England or northern New England.

DIPHTHONGS

ai	haalaiyi	(to be happy)	aisle
oi	chongoi	(his own pipe)	hoist
öi	ngöita	(to chase)	
ui	huilawu	(to distribute)	
aw	awta	(bow)	how
ew	pew'i	(come here)	
iw	piw	(again)	
uw	puwi	(to sleep)	

When w is the second element in a diphthong it has the value of a ue in a German word like tuer. It never occurs as a pure vowel. It is similar to the vowel sound of English words like few, pew, or cue, as they are pronounced in southern England or northern New England.

Hopi vowels may be either short or long in duration. When they are long, the letter is doubled to indicate it. This never affects the quality of the vowel. Thus, in English the a in bat is short in duration in contrast to the a in bad which is long.

| e | pep | (there) | is a short e |
| ee | peep | (almost) | is a long e |

CONSONANTS

p	pahu	(spring)	spot
t	tootim	(boys)	stop
k	kihu	(house)	sky

These three consonants are all unaspirated. Hopi lacks the related voiced consonants b, d, and g. When these sounds occur in initial position in a word they will sound similar to b, d, and g to one accustomed to English speech sounds.

| q | qöqa | (older sister) |

This sound is similar to the k, but contact is made with the back of the tongue and the velum rather than with the middle portion or the tongue and the palate as in a k.

h	hohu	(arrow)	how
l	loloma	(good)	low
m	mana	(girl)	many

| n | nonova | (to eat) | now |
| r | kyaro | (parrot) | |

The Hopi r does not occur in English. It is retroflex. That is, the tongue is curled up so that the under portion of the tongue is close to the palate. This gives the r a fricative quality that sounds like the z in azure.

| s | suukya | (one) |

The Hopi s is the unvoiced equivalent of the r. It is retroflex and produced in the same way as the r, except that the larynx or voice box does not function. This sound seems more like sh in some words, depending upon the vowels that precede or follow it. For this reason, it has been written sh in such contexts to facilitate reading, even though technically s and sh are one sound in Hopi.

| v | ivava | (my elder brother) voice |

The Hopi v is produced with both lips rather than with lips and teeth as in English. It is the same as a Spanish v. It is related to p, and all p's become v's when they occur between vowels. For example, piiva (tobacco) becomes iviiva (my tobacco).

| w | wuuti | (woman) | worry |
| y | yaqa | (nose) | you |

70

DIGRAPHS

Digraphs are single sounds represented by a combination of two letters. Since, English uses digraphs extensively, it was thought wiser to use the same combinations in Hopi in preference to introducing new symbols not found in the English alphabet.

ch chongo　　　(pipe)　　　　church

This sound in Hopi is unaspirated like the p, t, and k, making it sound similar to the j in judge to an ear accustomed to English speech sounds. In some villages a ts is substituted for the ch, especially in women's speech, and the example above would sound like tsongo.

ng ngahu　　　(medicine)　　sing

This sound is exactly the same as in English, but it can occur as the first sound in a word, whereas in English it is always intermediate or final.

ny honnyam	(bear clan)	new
		British or New England pronunciation
kw kwahu	(eagle)	question
ky tookyep	(all night)	cue
sh kyashnyam	(parrot clan)	shoe

See the discussion of s, of which this is a variant.